MONKEY'S LOOSE TOOTH

David Martin ILLUSTRATED BY Scott Nash

Introduction

Before your child starts reading, read this story
description. Then look through the book together
and talk about the pictures.

**This story is called *Monkey's Loose
Tooth*. It's about how Monkey pulls
his loose tooth and Mom pulls it too,
until he finally finds a way to get it out.**

Monkey pulls his tooth.

Mom pulls it too.

Monkey pulls his tooth.

Mom pulls it too.

Monkey pulls his tooth again.

Monkey gets an apple.

Monkey bites the apple.

Monkey smiles.